MOO LA LA!

Cow Goes Shopping

*To the
beautiful bovines
of Tillamook County – SS*

*To Mum, Bella &
Miss Daisy – BM*

SIMON AND SCHUSTER
First published in Great Britain in 2017 by Simon and Schuster UK Ltd
1st Floor, 222 Gray's Inn Road, London, WC1X 8HB • A CBS Company
Text copyright © 2017 Stephanie Shaw • Illustrations copyright © 2017 Becka Moor
The right of Stephanie Shaw and Becka Moor to be identified as the author
and illustrator of this work has been asserted by them in accordance with the
Copyright, Designs and Patents Act, 1988 • All rights reserved, including the right of
reproduction in whole or in part in any form • A CIP catalogue record for this book is
available from the British Library upon request.
978-1-4711-2339-9 (HB) • 978-1-4711-2340-5 (PB) • 978-1-4711-2341-2 (eBook)
Printed in China • 10 9 8 7 6 5 4 3 2 1

MOO LA LA!
Cow Goes Shopping

Stephanie Shaw & Becka Moor

SIMON & SCHUSTER

London   New York   Sydney   Toronto   New Delhi

Pete filled Cow's trough with water.
He fluffed her straw and set a bucket
of grain nearby.

"There you go, Cow," said Pete. "I'm going to do some errands in town. I'll be back by milking time. Come on, Dog, jump in the truck and let's go."

"It's not fair," bawled Cow. "I never get to ride in the truck. *Moo hoo!*"

"Think about it, Cow," said Pete. "It's a long ride in the back."

But Cow insisted she sat in the front with Pete and Dog.

"*Sour cream!*" she mooed. "*Are we there yet?*"

When they got to town, Pete told Dog and Cow to wait in the truck.

"I want to get away before that parade traffic hits. I won't be long. I need to buy some shoes for Horse."

MOO 1A 1A

"**What?** Horse has shoes?
I _never_ get to have shoes," bawled Cow.

"_Moo hoo! I want shoes toooo!_"

"Think about it, Cow," said Pete.
"You might not like shoes."

"Moo la la! I want those!"

Cow pointed a hoof at the shoe shop window.

It took a bit of doing, but Cow squeezed into two pairs of glittery red high-heels.

They had cute peep-toes, but they pinched her hooves until her eyes watered.

"Sweet yoghurt in the morning!"
Cow bellowed.

"How does Horse stand these things?"

"Let's move along now, Cow, the streets are filling up," said Pete, "and the missus wants me to buy some dressing for Turkey."

"*How come?*" asked Cow.

"Well, we always dress the turkey for dinner," Pete replied.

"*Mooo hooo!*" bawled Cow.

"*Then I want a dress too!*"

She wobbled along
until she came to
Moomingdales
Department Store.

"Good afternoon, Madame," said the sales assistant. "Might I interest you in a nice floral dress? It's even called a muumuu. It would be divine on you!"

"*Noooooooo!*" said Cow. "*I want that one!*"
"Think about it, Cow," said Pete. "It looks a little . . . ah . . . small."

"*But I want it,*" mooed Cow.

So a crew of salespeople buttoned, hooked
and zipped Cow into the dress.

"Hole-eee cheese on a cracker!" gasped Cow.

"How does Turkey breathe at dinner let alone eat!

I can hardly moooooove!"

"We **really** need to get going," said Pete.
"I just need to get some shears to trim sheep's coat."

"*What?* Sheep has a coat? What kind of coat?"

"Well, wool, of course."

"Moo hoo! Then I want a wool coat!" said Cow.

"No, Cow. Trust me. You will not like it," said Pete.
But Cow stamped her hooves and tossed her horns.

"Moo hoo! I need it! I want it!

I have to have it!"
she yelled.

And with that she charged up the escalator and stampeded through the china department.

She only stopped when she came to a whole flock of wool coats.

"*Moo la la! I want that one!*"
she said, pointing to a coat that already
had another wearer.

She tottered out of the shop in her brand new coat.

"*Merciful milkmaids!*" she bellowed.

"This thing itches my hide!"

"Cow, that's it. We **must** move along," said Pete.

By now Cow was too tired to climb into the front of the truck.

As Pete drove through town, the traffic slowed.

"Moo hoo!" cried Cow from the back.

"Mooo hoooooo!

My hooves hurt!

This dress is too tight on my tummies!

And this coat is mmmmmmiserable!"

The people lining the pavements stared
and pointed as Cow slowly went by.

When they reached the town square,
a woman rushed up to Pete.

"Oh my goodness!" she gushed. "You win the prize for . . ."

Best Dressed Bovine!

But when the rosette was placed on Cow's neck,
it was the final straw.

Her knees buckled. Her eyes rolled and she fainted.

When she woke up she was back on the farm.

Pete filled her trough with water, fluffed her straw
and set a bucket of grain nearby.

"Oh Pete, I was so *foolish*," said Cow.

"I'm going to stop asking for things I don't know anything about."

"I'm glad to hear that, Cow," said Pete.
"Now get some sleep. I need to put a ring on Bull."

"What? Bull has a ring?"

"Think about it, Cow," said Pete . . .

"You might not like it."